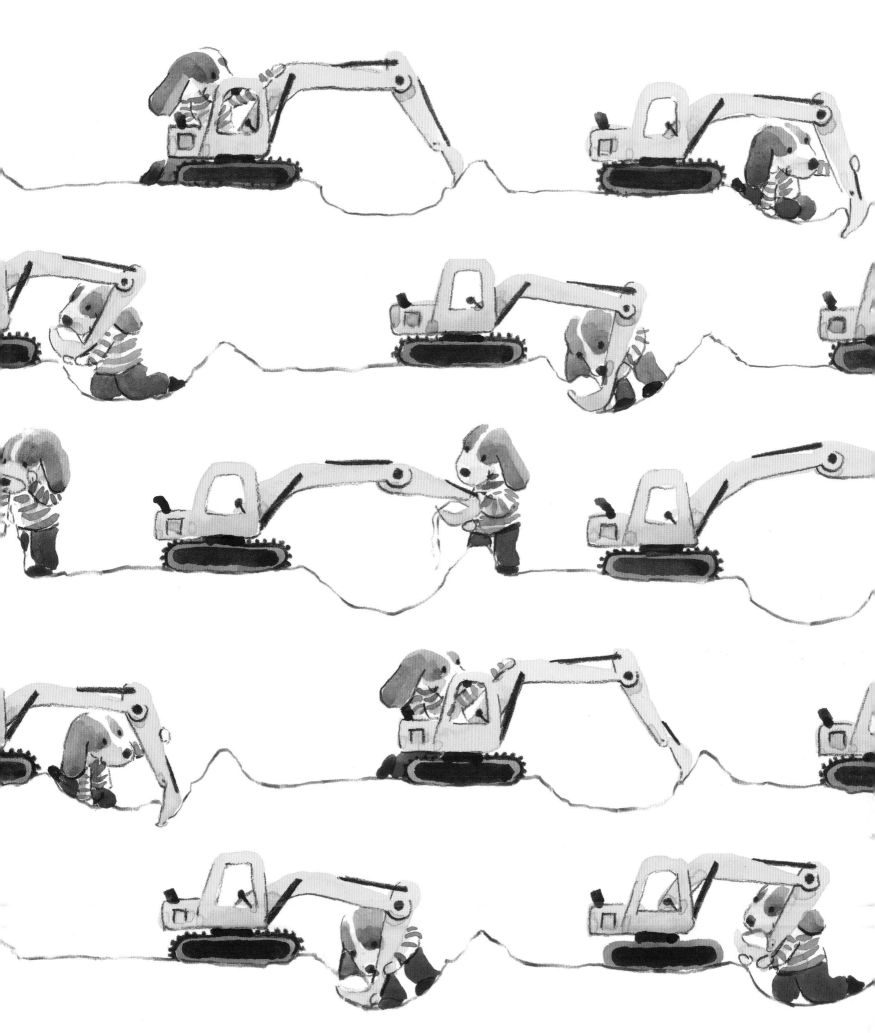

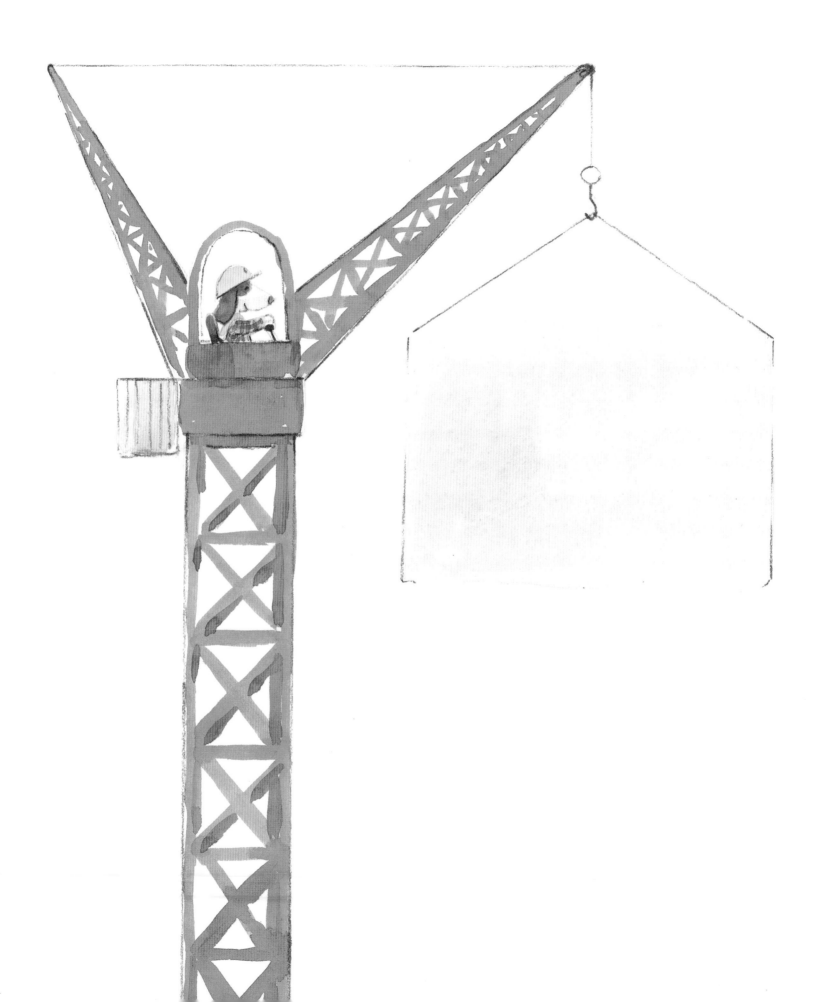

For Dennis, the best daddy I know!
C.A.

 little bee books

An imprint of Bonnier Publishing Group
853 Broadway, New York, New York 10003
Copyright © 2016 by Claire Alexander
First published in Great Britain by Egmont UK Limited.
This little bee books edition, 2016.
All rights reserved, including the right of
reproduction in whole or in part in any form.
LITTLE BEE BOOKS is a trademark of Bonnier Publishing Group,
and associated colophon is a trademark of Bonnier Publishing Group.
Manufactured in Malaysia 1215
First Edition 10 9 8 7 6 5 4 3 2 1
Library of Congress Cataloging-in-Publication Data
is available upon request.
ISBN 978-1-4998-0196-5
littlebeebooks.com
bonnierpublishing.com

The Best Part of
Daddy's Day

Claire Alexander

little bee books

My name is Bertie, and my daddy is a builder. He drives diggers and trucks every day!

Today he's going to go up in his crane and build a tall tower. When I'm big, I want to be a builder just like him . . .

. . . but right now I'm little, so I go to school.

Daddy drops me off on his way to work. "Have a good day, Bertie!" he says.

When the bell goes
BRRRIIING,
I run into class.

"Good morning, everyone," says my teacher.
"Today we're going to be builders."

This is going to be a great day!

First she reads us an exciting story about a digger.

Then I paint a picture of
a crane like Daddy's.
But someone spoils it . . .

and at lunchtime I trip and fall.

I wish I could see my daddy.

So I run to the playground
and go up, up, UP . . .

. . . to the top of the jungle gym. I'm so high up I can see the top of Daddy's tower!

There's someone inside
the crane—it must be him!

In the afternoon we all build an enormous tower.

I'm the small crane, and we let our teacher

be the big crane because she's wearing

the tallest shoes.

Our tower is amazing!

When school lets out, Daddy picks me up and gives me his hat to keep my ears dry. I tell him that I was a builder today, and the best part was making a tower, just like him.

Then I tell him about the not-so-good parts of my day—my spoiled painting and tripping and falling.

"I bet things like that never happen to you, Daddy," I say.

"Well, actually . . ."

"... they do sometimes!" says Daddy.

"Today someone spoiled
my brand new floor,

and I tripped and fell at lunchtime, just like you!"

"But then I finished my tower, and I think I saw you, Bertie, on the jungle gym!"

"It WAS me, Daddy!" I say, and I ask him if the best part of his day was finishing the tower.

"Actually, the best part of my day is right now," says Daddy, "being here with you, Bertie."

I snuggle up with Daddy and say, "I think **this** is the best part of my day, too."